D0045276

HaRD-BoiLED BUgS FoR BReAkFAST

Jack Prelutsky

HaRD-BOiLED BUgS FoR BReAkFAsT

And Other Tasty Poems

DRAWINGS BY
Ruth Chan

Greenwillow Books
An Imprint of HarperCollinsPublishers

Hard-Boiled Bugs for Breakfast
Text copyright © 2021 by Jack Prelutsky;
illustrations copyright © 2021 by Ruth Chan

The text of this book is set in 14-point Sabon.
Book design by Paul Zakris

Library of Congress Cataloging-in-Publication
Data is available.

ISBN 9780063019133 (hardback)

21 22 23 24 25 PC/LSCH 10 9 8 7 6 5 4 3 2 1
First Edition

 Greenwillow Books

To Susan Hirschman

Hard-Boiled Bugs for Breakfast

Hard-boiled bugs for breakfast,
Hard-boiled bugs for lunch,
Hard-boiled bugs at suppertime,
Crunchy! Crunchy! Crunch!

Hard-boiled bugs are tastier
Than spiders, flies, or slugs.
There's not a doubt about it—
I love those hard-boiled bugs.

If Butterflies Baked Cherry Pies

If butterflies baked cherry pies,
And lemons were not sour,
If baseball bats turned into cats,
And seconds took an hour,
If bumblebees made cottage cheese,
And ice cream was red-hot,
I doubt that I would wonder why
I was confused a lot.

A Giant Easter Bunny

A giant Easter Bunny
Is parading down my street.
Its ears are quite spectacular,
It has stupendous feet.
It has a merry twinkle
In its two enormous eyes.
I never thought a bunny
Could be even half that size.

It's a prepossessing bunny,
Fully more than ten feet tall.
The clamor would be deafening
If ever it should fall.
I'm glad that Easter Bunny
Has a pair of sturdy legs,
For if it took a tumble
It might scramble all its eggs.

My Lizard

My lizard plays the mandolin,
Although not very well.
My frog drums out of rhythm
On my turtle's shiny shell.

My turtle tries its best to sing,
But only squawks a lot.
I wish my pets were talented—
Apparently, they're not.

My Elephant

My elephant is tinted pink
With purple polka dots.
My elephant has taught herself
To tie her trunk in knots.
My elephant turns somersaults
A dozen times a day.
My elephant eats hardly half
A teaspoonful of hay.

My elephant can use her tail
To play the violin.
Her voice is sweet, so when she sings
I always join right in.
My elephant is not a chore
To keep around at all.
My lovely little elephant
Is only one inch tall.

My Clock

I have an odd, contrary clock
That doesn't really work.
I've more or less determined
That it's basically berserk.
It makes some disconcerting sounds,
As though its parts are loose,
And when it comes to telling time,
My clock is of no use.

Sometimes my clock runs backward,
Sometimes it's fast . . . or slow,
Sometimes it doesn't run at all,
I simply never know.
Sometimes it tocks but doesn't tick,
Or ticks but doesn't tock.
My clock keeps going cuckoo,
Though it's not a cuckoo clock.

Today When I Got Out of Bed

Today when I got out of bed
I noticed right away
That I was two feet taller,
And my hair had turned to hay.
My nose looked like a tangerine,
My toes were four feet long,
My fingers all had feathers—
There was clearly something wrong.

I felt a little hungry,
So I ate ten loaves of bread,
Eleven bowls of cereal,
Which turned my ears bright red.
I also ate an elephant,
And drank a swimming pool.
I've only one more thing to say,
And that is . . . April Fool!

My Family's Last Picnic

At my family's last picnic
We knew at a glance,
We'd soon be invaded
By armies of ants.
They swarmed over tree trunks,
They marched over rocks,
And soon found our blankets,
Our shoes, and our socks.

They ate all our crackers,
Our chicken and cheese,
They swallowed our burgers
With nonchalant ease.
They ate all our hot dogs,
Including the mustard,
Then downed our bananas
And coconut custard.

Those ravenous ants
Were exceedingly rude,
And didn't depart
Till they'd finished our food.
A picnic does not
Stand a ghost of a chance,
When it's at the mercy
Of merciless ants.

The Leaves Are Drifting

The leaves are drifting to the ground,
I'm thoroughly ecstatic.
They do that every single fall . . .
It's sort of autumn-atic.

I Turn the Rain On

I turn the rain on with my key,
And soon it showers merrily.
I let it rain till I'm as wet
As anyone can ever get.

And that is when I softly sigh,
And wish that I could now be dry.
It also is the moment when
I turn the rain back off again.

The Kangarooster

The KANGAROOSTER does not yawn
When it arises, right at dawn.
Instead, as if to spread the news,
It loudly cock-a-doodle-doos.
When it's awakened everyone
In time to see the morning sun,
It puffs its chest and pecks the air,
Then struts about with pride and flair.

When these proceedings are complete,
It springs away on giant feet.
With every monumental bound,
It covers yards and yards of ground.
As it continues down the trail,
It flourishes its massive tail.
Then, with one final mighty leap,
It yawns at last, and falls asleep.

kang-uh-ROO-ster

The Stir-Frying Pandas

The STIR-FRYING PANDAS, with little ado,
Fry succulent shoots of the finest bamboo.
Their system is simple, yet somehow complete . . .
They eat all they fry, and they fry all they eat.

The STIR-FRYING PANDAS are quiet and shy.
They'll probably vanish if you happen by.
It's only a fortunate few who have viewed
The STIR-FRYING PANDAS preparing their food.

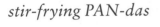

stir-frying PAN-das

If the Moon

If the moon were a balloon,
We would hardly have to wait
For the moon to disappear . . .
It might suddenly deflate.
If the moon were made of cheese,
As some people used to think,
It would be a dreadful place,
And would definitely stink.

If the moon were fiery hot,
A bright, miniature sun,
All the creatures of this Earth
Would be thoroughly well-done.
But the moon is not a sun,
Neither cheese nor great balloon—
We are happy to report
That the moon is just the moon.

My Nose

I'm happy that my nose is short,
And not twelve inches long,
For then my nose would be a foot—
That would be very wrong.

My Dragon Is Mad at My Ogre

My dragon is mad at my ogre,
My ogre is mad at my gnome,
My gnome will not talk to my goblin.
It's truly upsetting my home.

My goblin despises my griffin,
My griffin can't stomach my troll,
And nobody cares for my gargoyle. . . .
It's all a great rigmarole.

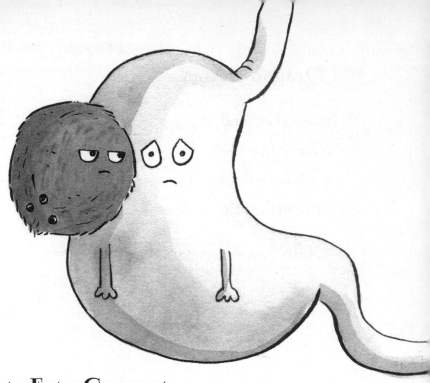

I Tried to Eat a Coconut

I tried to eat a coconut,
But I did something wrong.
My stomach and that coconut
Just didn't get along.

It gave me indigestion,
And I'm still not feeling well.
Next time I eat a coconut,
I'll first remove the shell.

If I Had No Homework

If I had no homework,
By that I mean NEVER,
I wouldn't complain
About anything . . . ever.
I'm certain I wouldn't
Shed one single tear
If homework were banished
Throughout the whole year.

If I had no homework,
My heart would be lighter,
My mood would be sunny,
My smile would be brighter.
I'd leap in the air
And I'd happily shout. . . .
But no! I have homework,
There's just no way out.

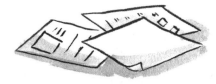

I've Got a Cold

I've got a cold,
I've got the flu.
I'm stuck with mumps,
And measles too.
I've got a fever
And a chill.
It's clear that I'm
Extremely ill.

My stomach's full
Of pointy rocks,
And also I've got
Chicken pox,
And if you look,
You're sure to find
A ghastly rash
On my behind.

I'm suffering
From frozen toes,
And something's stopping
Up my nose.
My throat is sore,
I cough and cough.

My head feels ready
To fly off.
My chest is wet,
My mouth is dry,
It almost makes me
Want to cry.
I'm miserable
In every way . . .
I think I should
Skip school today.

I Planted an Eggplant

I planted an eggplant
To grow an egg,
But all I grew
Was a table leg.

I planted that leg
To grow a bowl,
But all I grew
Was a lump of coal.

I planted that coal
To grow a pail,
But all I grew
Was a rusty nail.

I planted that nail
To grow a clock,
But all I grew
Was a smelly sock.

I planted that sock
To grow a suit,
But all I grew
Was a broken flute.

I planted that flute
To grow a wall,
But all I grew
Was a basketball.

I'll never plant
That basketball,
For that would make
No sense at all.

Figure 8

It seems to be my endless fate to navigate this figure eight for there is nowhere else to go as far as I can tell, and so

Above a Meadow

Above a meadow, sneezing bees
Have sneezed and sneezed for hours.
Those sneezing bees have allergies. . . .
They're allergic to the flowers.

My Bike Has No Pedals

My bike has no pedals,
My skates have no wheels,
My shirt's full of holes,
And my shoes have no heels.
My model car broke,
And my bell doesn't ring,
My table is wobbly,
My kite has no string.

My belt has no buckle,
My cap is too tight,
My gloves have no thumbs,
And my lamp doesn't light.
My brush has no bristles,
My baseball is worn,
My books have no pages,
Their covers are torn.

My teaspoon is bent,
And my dish has a chip,
My clock will not run,
And my zippers won't zip.
Though some people say
That I've not got a lot,
I'm perfectly happy
With what I have got.

I'm Allergic to My Puppy

I'm allergic to my puppy,
He makes me sneeze and sneeze.
I'm allergic to my kitten,
She routinely makes me wheeze.
I'm allergic to my gerbil,
He makes me cough a lot.
I'm allergic to my turtle,
She makes my head feel hot.

When I'm around my bunny,
I erupt in tiny bumps.
My chicken makes me itchy,
And my lizard gives me lumps.
When I am near my parakeet
My forehead sweats and sweats.
Sometimes I almost wonder
If I've one too many pets.

The Skigulls

Silently the SKIGULLS glide
Down the snowy mountainside,
Swift and graceful, at their ease,
Masters of their built-in skis.

At the bottom of the hill,
They're unlikely to stay still.
To the top the SKIGULLS soar. . . .
Soon they'll ski the slopes once more.

SKEE-gullz

On the Last Day of December

On the last day of December,
Just before I went to sleep,
I made some resolutions
That I promised I would keep.

I would never take my crayons
And draw pictures on the wall.
I would not allow my lizards
To run loose around the hall.

I would finish all my spinach,
Though it really is the worst,
And I'd never hit my sister,
Even if she hit me first.

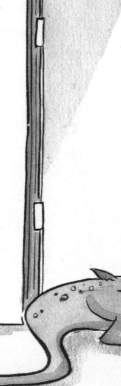

I would take my muddy boots off
When I tramped into the house,
And I wouldn't scare my mother
With my hamster or my mouse.

I would wash my dirty face
Until it sparkled like the sun. . . .
Now it's January second,
And I've broken every one.

Oh Orioleander

Oh ORIOLEANDER,
How beautiful you are.
Your plumage is exquisite,
You shimmer like a star.
We love your tail of blossoms
Ablaze with red and white.
Oh ORIOLEANDER,
You are a splendid sight.

Oh ORIOLEANDER,
How wondrous you appear.
Your fragrance is entrancing,
Your song enthralls the ear.
You always cheer our spirits
As you prepare your nest.
Oh ORIOLEANDER,
We wish you all the best.

aw-ree-oh-lee-AN-dur

I Baked a Cake of Sunlight

I baked a cake of sunlight
But didn't like the taste.
I baked a cake of rainbows,
The colors went to waste.

I baked a cake of moonbeams
And hated every bite.
I baked a cake of flour and eggs—
The flavor is just right.

My Carrots Are Angry

My carrots are angry,
My scallions are sore.
My beans are so mad
They can't laugh anymore.
My radishes sulk,
And my artichokes fret.
My pumpkins are peeved,
And my peas are upset.

My cabbages grumble,
My broccoli glares.
My onions are sullen,
My celery stares.
Confounded, confused,
I don't know what to do
When all of my vegetables
Are in a stew.

Duck

Happily I quack.
Water bounces off my back.
It's my special knack.

Lion

I don't join the hunt,
Yet get the biggest portion.
It's good to be king.

Pig

When I roll in mud,
No creature in the barnyard
Is half as happy.

Bat

I slumber all day
Upside down in deep darkness.
The night sky is mine.

Turtle

I know that I'm slow,
But, sandwiched between two shells,
It's hard to hurry.

Whale

I am gigantic.
When I burst through the surface,
I spout a geyser.

I Dove into a Chocolate Lake

I dove into a chocolate lake,
And swam for half a day,
That's why I smell like chocolate,
And the smell won't go away.

I'm not the least bit bothered
By my rich aroma now,
For if I had my choice, I'd smell
Like chocolate anyhow.

The Fnatt

The Fnatt has four enormous eyes,
With which it cries and cries and cries.
As doleful as a beast can be,
It sobs and sobs incessantly.

It has no reason to express
Such infinite unhappiness.
It's just the nature of the Fnatt—
Some people are a lot like that.

I'm Mad at the Baker

I'm mad at the baker,
He sold me a cake
That tasted like fish heads
And pieces of snake,
Like plaster of paris
Plus elephant trunks,
With flavors from donkeys,
Gorillas, and skunks.

I tried to return it
The following day,
But that baker was nasty
And snarled, "Go away."
He sampled a piece,
And exclaimed with a smile,
"This cake is delicious!"
I answered, "It's vile!"

"Your cake tastes of blubber,
And porcupine quills,
Of pelican bellies,
And platypus bills,
Plus rotten potato peels,
Overcooked peas,
Of bicycle tires,
And smelly old cheese.

"It's the very worst cake
You could possibly bake,
A cake you could only
Create by mistake.
Please, please take it back."
"Never! Never!" he said.
That's why he's now wearing
That cake on his head.

I Am Lighter Than a Feather

I am lighter than a feather,
Twice as heavy as a whale.
I am swifter than a cheetah,
Even slower than a snail.
I'm as sour as a lemon,
And as sweet as sugarcane,
I am drier than a desert,
And as wet as falling rain.

I am noisier than thunder,
And as silly as a clown.
I am happier than laughter,
I am sadder than a frown.
I'm as golden as a sunbeam,
And as silver as the moon,
I'm as smooth as silk or satin,
And as wrinkled as a prune.

I'm as silent as a shadow
And as clever as a fox.
I am braver than a lion,
I am stronger than an ox.
I am steeper than a mountain,
I am deeper than the sea.
Yes, the more I think about it,
I am positively me.

My Cow

My cow sits on a maple bough,
I don't know why, I don't know how.
She wears a gown of yellow silk,
And once a day gives chocolate milk.

Fantelopes

FANTELOPES have just one rule,
And that's to try and keep you cool.
Accomplishing this simple task
Is all these gentle creatures ask.

FANTELOPES, you may be sure,
Will soon reduce your temperature.
Then, having done the best they can,
They look for someone else to fan.

FAN-tih-lopes

The Poor Revolving Doormouse

The poor REVOLVING DOORMOUSE
Is in such an awful bind.
It cannot keep from spinning,
And pursuing its behind.
Each time it travels faster
Than the time it did before.
How can that hapless creature
Hope to bear it anymore?

The poor REVOLVING DOORMOUSE
Is indeed in dreadful shape,
Embroiled in a predicament
From which there's no escape.
If only it could slow itself
For just the slightest spell . . .
But sadly, it accelerates—
Things may not turn out well.

re-VOL-ving DOOR-mouse

OW!

I am
OW! OW!
sitting
OW! OW!
on a
cactus
OW! OW! OW!
just to see
if I could sit
while being stuck.
OW! OW! OW! OW!
Now I'd like to leave
OW! OW!
but I don't know
OW! OW! how.
I am OW! OW!
out of OW! OW!
OW! OW! OW! OW!
OW! OW! luck.

My Kitchen Was Invaded

My kitchen was invaded
By a horde of nibbling mice.
They nibbled, nibbled, nibbled
On my peanuts, cheese, and rice.

I built a better mousetrap
To remove them from my house.
It didn't do a single thing—
They've made a better mouse.

The World's Most Intelligent Chicken

The world's most intelligent chicken,
As well as the world's wisest duck,
Were challenged to take an IQ test—
They agreed with a quack and a cluck.
For fowl that were rated so highly,
Their knowledge turned out to be small.
In fact, it was quickly apparent
They knew nearly nothing at all.

They thought that an ibis had petals,
They thought that an iris had wings.
They thought that potatoes grew feathers,
They thought that a cantaloupe sings.
They thought that a floor needed windows,
That apples grew under the sea,
That clocks always ran counterclockwise,
And eight minus seven was three.

They struggled with every last question
On science, math, music, and art.
You'd never suspect, from their answers,
That they were supposed to be smart.
They filled in the blanks incorrectly,
Their two little brains remained stuck. . . .
A chicken is only a chicken,
A duck is no more than a duck.

No No No

No no no, I'm not around,
I am nowhere to be found.
Have I simply disappeared?
The experience is weird.

If I'm neither here nor there,
Am I even anywhere?
It's a most disturbing plight
To be dropping out of sight.

It concerns me very much
That I'm truly out of touch.
I believe that, recently,
I was who I used to be.

Can I go back anymore
To the me I was before?
This dilemma makes me sigh.
That's enough for now . . . goodbye!

Bubble

Jane the Complainer

I'm Jane the Complainer,
I love to complain,
I complain in the sun,
I complain in the rain.
I complain when it's cold,
I complain when it's hot,
I complain when it's windy,
And when it is not.

I complain when it's quiet,
And when it is loud.
I complain when alone,
I complain in a crowd.
I complain every day,
I complain every night.
I complain in the dark,
I complain in the light.

I complain on a bus,
I complain on a train,
I complain on a boat,
I complain on a plane.
I complain to the trees,
To the flowers and rocks,
I complain to my shoes,
I complain to my socks.

I complain to the ceiling,
The floor, and the wall.
I even complain
Over nothing at all.
From constant complaining
I fail to refrain.
I'm Jane the Complainer,
I love to complain.

The Limber Rubber Bandicoot

The limber RUBBER BANDICOOT
Cavorts in its elastic suit,
Exhibiting, for all to see,
Its famous flexibility.
It soon expands, before our eyes,
To more than twice its normal size,
Proceeding then to bend and twist
In ways too numerous to list.

It deftly stretches more and more,
Till it's much larger than before,
And soon appears so thin and flat,
It's basically a rubber mat.
It then snaps back, becoming small,
And forms itself into a ball
That bounces, as we all salute
That limber RUBBER BANDICOOT.

ruh-burr-BAN-dih-coot

Bananas

I only eat bananas
When I am upside down.
I can't digest an apple
Unless I wear my crown.
I will not swallow waffles
Until I blow my nose,
And never eat tomatoes
Until my rooster crows.

I only eat potatoes
When I am up a tree,
And eating peas on weekends
Is impossible for me.
If I don't wear a sweater,
I can't eat a single bean,
And if it isn't Tuesday,
I can't touch a tangerine.

I never dine on carrots
Until I take a nap,
And cannot stomach peanuts
Unless I swim a lap.
I can't have avocadoes
Unless I'm smeared with jam,
But I can feast on chocolate
Exactly as I am.

My Friends and I Went Bowling

My friends and I went bowling,
But we did not score at all.
Although we tried our hardest,
Not a single pin would fall.

I wonder . . . was the ball too light,
And just a bit too small?
The next time we go bowling,
We won't use a Ping-Pong ball.

The Crabbits

The CRABBITS inhabit the meadows,
The CRABBITS inhabit the beach.
If you should encounter a CRABBIT,
Be sure to stay out of its reach.
Although they appear to be harmless,
It's not necessarily so,
There's something outrageous about them,
It's something that's handy to know.

The CRABBITS have one little habit,
For which they are nicely designed—
To silently sneak up beside you,
And suddenly nip your behind.
You'll hop in the air if it happens,
You'll holler, you'll yammer, you'll screech.
Take note when you stroll through the meadows,
Beware when you wander the beach.

CRAB-its

I Threw Myself a Party

I threw myself a party
To surprise myself today,
Inviting friends I did not know,
Who promised not to stay.
We played a few confusing games,
For which we did not care,
Then ate unpleasant party snacks
That simply weren't there.

Since it was no one's birthday,
It was hardly a mistake
To not blow out the candles
On the nonexistent cake.
We sang some songs that no one knew,
So didn't make a sound,
Then opened all my presents,
That were nowhere to be found.

We tried our hand at hide-and-seek,
Though none of us would hide,
Then raced and raced around the yard,
Yet always stayed inside.
Since everyone was someone
That I still don't recognize,
My party was successful,
And a wonderful surprise.

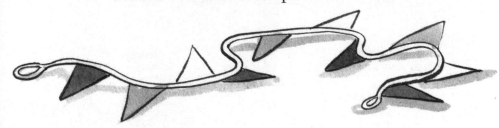

I Looked Out My Window

I looked out my window,
And what did I see?
A purple rhinoceros
Waving to me,
A flying baboon
In a big floppy hat,
A laughing giraffe
Half the size of a cat.

I looked a while longer,
And what did I spy?
A kangaroo baking
A coconut pie,
A pair of pink pigs
Wearing polka-dot pants,
Performing a graceful
And intricate dance.

I saw many things
I can never forget,
An elephant playing
A huge clarinet—
The view from my window
Is clearly the way
To see wondrous things
I don't see every day.

A Groundhog Speaks

Why must these people waken me?
Why won't they let me sleep,
And dream my little groundhog dreams
Of tunnels dark and deep?
It's February second,
And they've pulled me from my bed.
They do this to me every year—
I should have planned ahead.

It's all about my shadow,
Which they think may let them know
If winter will remain awhile
Or pack its bags and go.
Why can't they check the shadow
Of a chicken or a sheep?
I wish it weren't Groundhog Day. . . .
I really need my sleep.

Thanksgiving Dinner

The food is on the table,
And the turkey came out tough.
The stuffing's a catastrophe,
It wasn't cooked enough.
The green beans are so overdone
They're practically gray,
The yams are much too mushy,
Someone left them on all day.

Cousin Judy keeps complaining
That there's something in her eye,
Uncle Rudy broke a mirror
When he tried to swat a fly.
Aunt Jeanette has started sneezing,
And she cannot seem to stop,
Cousin Dotty dropped the salad,
Aunt Marie has got the mop.

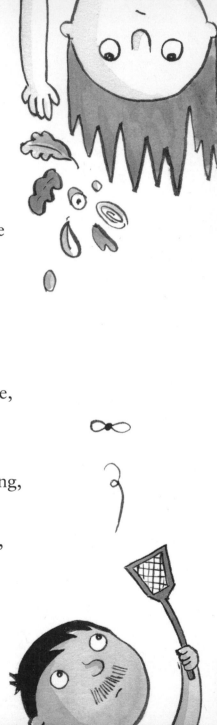

Aunt Bertha's loudly babbling
Into Uncle Willie's ear,
Uncle Charlie's telling stories
That I'm not supposed to hear,
Cousin Michael made my father
A toupee of sauerkraut,
Cousin Rose is in the bathroom,
And refuses to come out.

The pumpkin pie is missing,
We can't find it anywhere,
Uncle Steve is sleeping soundly,
Snoring in an easy chair.
The baby's smearing gravy
On my mother's brand-new blouse—
I adore Thanksgiving dinner
At my grandma's cozy house.

I Found a Giant Apple

I found a giant apple
That had fallen from a tree.
I picked it up and took a bite,
It tasted fine to me.
I took another bite of it,
And then I bit some more.
I'd never had an apple
Even half this big before.

It also was delicious,
So I took another bite.
That's when I noticed something
That destroyed my appetite.
My face turned sour and sickly,
And I couldn't help but squirm,
As I learned the biggest apple
Also gets the biggest worm.

A Band of Trick-or-Treaters

A band of trick-or-treaters
Is heading for my door.
I spy a walking pizza,
A bright green dinosaur.
Here comes a knight in armor,
A horseman with no head,
A can of corn, a skeleton,
A living loaf of bread.

They trundle through my garden
In ragtag single file,
And when they ring my doorbell,
I greet them with a smile.
The second that they see me,
They scream and flee in fear—
It's clear they didn't realize
That Dracula lives here.

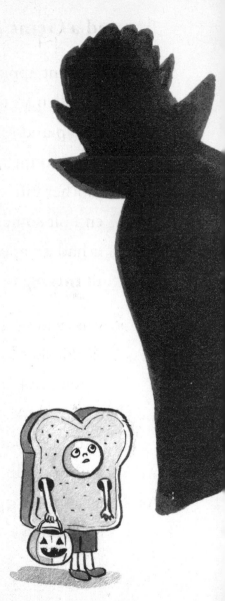

My Cows Have Stopped Mooing

My cows have stopped mooing,
My chickens don't cluck.
There's hardly a quack
Coming out of my duck.
My mouse's small squeak
Is diminished by half. . . .
They're all taking voice lessons
From my giraffe.

A Kitchen Sink

I am in a kitchen sink
And I don't know
What to think.
I suspect this is a place
I can't remain.
Now I'm frightened
And aghast,
For I'm falling very fast. . . .
I am swirling swirling
swirling
swirling swirling
swirling
d
o
w
n
t
h
e
d
r
a
i
n

The Hesitant Shrimpala

The hesitant SHRIMPALA
Is helpless to decide
If it should seek the forest,
Or plunge into the tide.
It's not designed for running,
It's ill-equipped to swim.
It's in a constant quandary,
Its destiny seems grim.

That maladroit SHRIMPALA
Can't seem to calculate
How it's supposed to function
In this mystifying state.
It stands and waits, immobile,
And never does a thing.
Life for the poor SHRIMPALA
Is quite bewildering.

shrim-PA-la

I'm Stuck to a Magnet

I'm stuck to a magnet
And cannot get loose.
I struggle and struggle . . .
So far it's no use.

I can't move a muscle,
I can't move a hair.
I'll never again
Put on steel underwear.

My Father Woke Us Early

My father woke us early.
"Get up! Get up!" he said.
"We'll have a picnic in the park,
So let's get out of bed.
It's Labor Day all day today,
A day that I hold dear,
A day we celebrate the work
That people do all year."

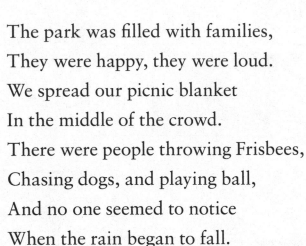

The park was filled with families,
They were happy, they were loud.
We spread our picnic blanket
In the middle of the crowd.
There were people throwing Frisbees,
Chasing dogs, and playing ball,
And no one seemed to notice
When the rain began to fall.

We swallowed soggy sandwiches
And sour lemonade.
Then Mother said, "Let's have dessert,
A special one I made."
A trillion ants trooped over it
And carried it away.
We all got drenched together—
What a lovely Labor Day.

If You Squeeze

If you squeeze electric eels,
You won't like the way it feels.
When they knock you off your block,
You'll be in a state of shock.

Once a Week at Noon

Once a week at noon,
I eat a neon sign
Without a fork or spoon—
Light lunches are divine.

We Are the Oceans

We are the oceans,
We are the land,
We are the mountains,
The rocks, and the sand.
We are the meadows,
The flowers and trees,
The delicate grasses
That sway in the breeze.

We are the thunder,
We are the storm,
The numberless insects
Of infinite form.
We are the furry ones
Flourishing tails.
We are the tigers,
We are the whales.

We are the creatures
With feather and fin,
We're every last being
That ever has been.
We're all of these things
On the world of our birth,
This wonderful planet,
Our beautiful Earth.

A Clam

A clam is a creature
Of quiet aplomb.
In all situations
A clam remains calm.
A clam doesn't wander
Or move very much. . . .
It's easy to think
That a clam's out of touch.

A clam doesn't care
To do dangerous deeds.
A quiet location
Is all a clam needs.
And so a clam rarely
Is subject to strife.
A clam simply *is*,
Which is not a bad life.

The Boxing Glove Birds

High in the treetops,
The BOXING GLOVE BIRDS
Are boxing each other all day.
They box and they box,
Never saying a word—
Of course, they have nothing to say.

They box and they box,
Yet they never get hurt,
For none of them hit very hard.
But nevertheless,
All those BOXING GLOVE BIRDS
Must constantly keep up their guard.

BOX-ing gluv-burdz

My Horse Is Floating in the Air

My horse is floating in the air
Above the tallest trees,
While I relax upon his back
And feel the morning breeze.

I don't know what his secret is,
But I am glad, of course,
To be the one who gets to ride
The only floating horse.

I've Always Loved Spaghetti

I've always loved spaghetti,
And considered it a treat.
There's never been another thing
That I would rather eat.
So one morning when I noticed
That my stock was running dry,
I decided to take measures
And replenish my supply.

I went mining for spaghetti
In the macaroni hills,
Using all the best equipment,
Hammers, chisels, picks, and drills.
I dug and dug around the clock,
I dug with all my might,
But spaghetti stayed elusive,
And remained out of my sight.

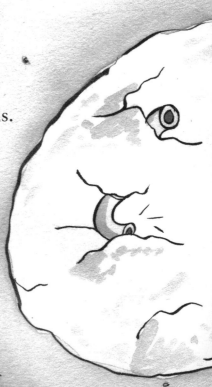

I've dug and dug for many years,
Through rock and clay and sand,
But I've never struck spaghetti,
Not a solitary strand.
But still I keep on digging,
Even now, when I've grown old.
I have yet to find spaghetti . . .
All I've ever found is gold.

If You Won't Be My Valentine

If you won't be my valentine,
Then this is what I'll do—
I'll dress up in banana peels,
And paint my stomach blue.

I'll glue tomatoes to my ears,
And swallow apple cores.
But if you'll be my valentine,
I promise I'll be yours.

My Garden Glows

My garden glows all evening.
My garden glows all night.
When people see my garden,
They gasp with pure delight.

It seems the bulbs I planted
In long and tidy rows
Are all electric light bulbs—
And so my garden glows.

The Octopus Octet

We're the famous octopuses
Of the Octopus Octet.
The combo that compares with us
Does not exist as yet.
Besides our fine musicianship,
We're deft at many stunts.
We play assorted instruments,
A horde of them at once.

We play oboes, basses, banjos,
Trumpets, cellos, and guitars,
Harmonicas, and xylophones,
We're utter superstars.
Our music has a quality
You simply can't forget.
We're the famous octopuses
Of the Octopus Octet.

The Bumblebeet

Behold the brazen BUMBLEBEET
That surely is not good to eat,
And furthermore, it likes to sting. . . .
It is a most annoying thing.

It's striped with gold and black and red,
And if it buzzes by your head,
You'd better make a quick retreat. . . .
Do not confront the BUMBLEBEET.

BUM-bull-beet

The Peculiar Coconuthatch

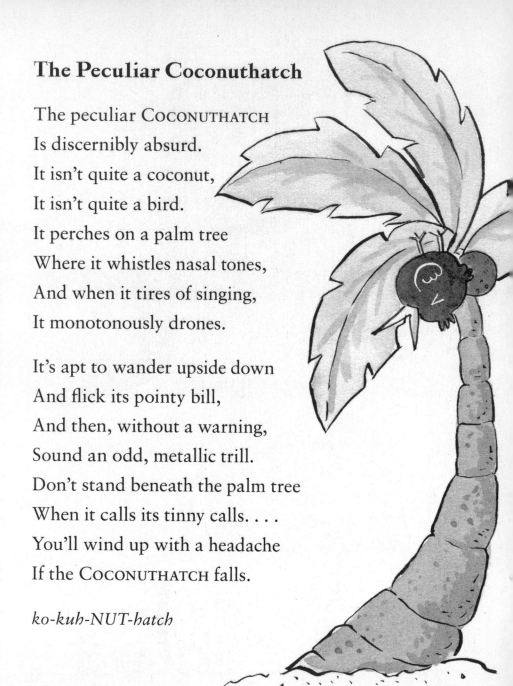

The peculiar COCONUTHATCH
Is discernibly absurd.
It isn't quite a coconut,
It isn't quite a bird.
It perches on a palm tree
Where it whistles nasal tones,
And when it tires of singing,
It monotonously drones.

It's apt to wander upside down
And flick its pointy bill,
And then, without a warning,
Sound an odd, metallic trill.
Don't stand beneath the palm tree
When it calls its tinny calls. . . .
You'll wind up with a headache
If the COCONUTHATCH falls.

ko-kuh-NUT-hatch

My Cockroach

I used to have a cockroach,
An insect with no peers,
A bug that was triumphant
For many, many years.
At racing and at wrestling,
My cockroach reigned supreme.
He was the sort of cockroach
About which people dream.

My cockroach was a champion,
A superstar, an ace.
In every competition,
He always won first place.
My cockroach was a wonder,
He was nimble, he was trim,
The finest cockroach ever
Till my sister stepped on him.

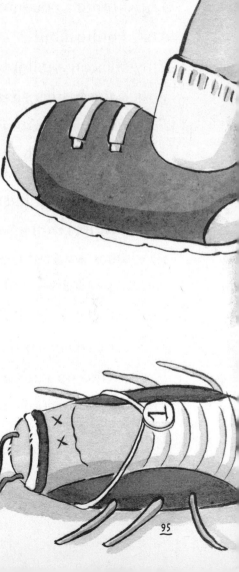

When the Clothing Got Together

When the clothing got together
For their yearly jamboree,
The shorts ran in a circle,
And the shirts sat down to tea.
The sweaters soon perspired,
Which the halters tried to stop.
The trunks were on the bottom,
And the hats were on the top.

The socks exchanged some punches,
And the belts threw punches too.
The skirts avoided issues,
While the briefs prepared to sue.
The boots thought they'd go hiking,
And the scarves all ate a lot.
The sneakers acted shifty,
And the tights were in a spot.

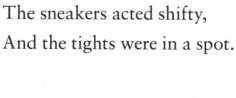

The jeans appeared unhappy
When the dresses wrote in code.
A pair of shoes was swaying,
And another hoped it snowed.
The robes went in the water,
And the suits began to leap.
The coats were acting petty,
The pajamas went to sleep.

The kilts announced, too loudly,
That the stole was just a crook.
The pants could not stop gasping,
And a jacket read a book.
The gloves teased one another,
And the slippers took a fall.
A sari begged their pardon,
But the caps all had a ball.

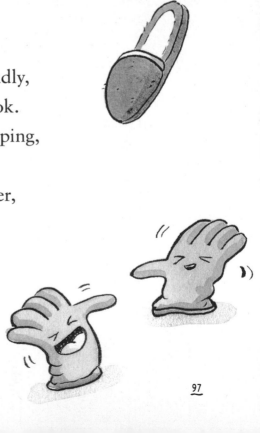

The Leemies

The Leemies won't leave us alone.
They nibble our noses all night.
Despite how we whimper and moan,
They nip and they peck and they bite.

We cannot control what they do.
A way to resist is unknown,
And so they continue to chew—
The Leemies won't leave us alone.

The World's Most Ancient Ant

I, the world's most ancient ant,
Am growing frail and weak.
What other ants can do, I can't—
I am an ant antique.

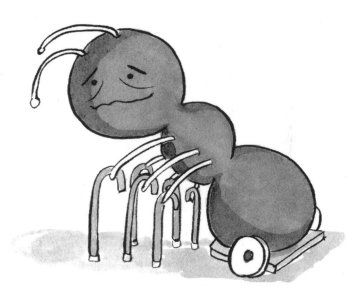

I Forgot

I forgot to eat my breakfast,
I forgot to wear my cap,
I forgot to take a shower,
I forgot to take a nap,
I forgot to kiss my mother,
I forgot to have my snack,
I forgot to ride my scooter,
I forgot to scratch my back.

I forgot to feed my turtle,
I forgot to comb my hair,
I forgot to put my socks on,
I forgot my underwear,
And I meant to do my homework,
But I totally forgot,
And I forgot some other things,
But I've forgotten what.

My Up Is Down

My up is down,
My down is up,
My cup's a plate,
My plate's a cup.
My spoon's a fork,
My fork's a spoon,
My baseball bat
Is a balloon.

My right is left,
My left is right,
The sun is coming
Out at night.
My smile appears
To be a frown,
Because my head
Is upside down.

My slow is fast,
My fast is slow,
My low is high,
My high is low.
My here is there,
My there is here,
My far away
Is very near.

My best is worst,
My worst is best,
My fish is in
A treetop nest.
My play is work,
My work is play. . . .
It's just that sort
Of day today.

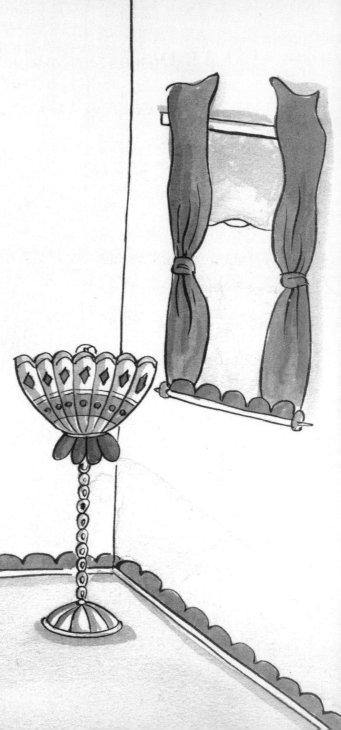

The Wazawa

I am the Wazawa,
I do as I please.
I breakfast on pickles,
Erasers, and fleas.
I stay up all night,
Often just out of spite,
And when I get tired,
I sneeze with delight.

I am the Wazawa,
I do as I choose.
I lunch on suspenders,
And smelly old shoes.
My afternoon snack
Is the fur of a yak,
Along with a slice
Of a trolley car track.

There's hardly a thing
I'm unwilling to eat.
A moldy old sponge
Is a marvelous treat.
I dine on dead trees
With unparalleled ease.
I am the Wazawa,
I do as I please.

If I Were King of Everything

If I were king of everything,
Which so far I am not,
My subjects would adore me
And would honor me a lot,
For I'd make sure that everyone
Had seven meals a day,
A pony and a tricycle,
A skateboard and a sleigh.

My subjects each would own at least
A hundred shoes and socks,
A pair of silk pajamas,
And a dozen cuckoo clocks.
And everyone would have a car,
An airplane, and a yacht,
If I were king of everything . . .
Which so far I am not.

I Love to Sleep All Morning

I love to sleep all morning,
I love to sleep all night,
And sleeping through the afternoon
Is truly my delight.

I simply yawn a little
And collapse into a heap,
Then do the thing that I do best . . .
I sleep and sleep and sleep.

Sludd

I'm known as Sludd,
I roll in mud.
I have no bones,
I have no blood.
My form is an
Imperfect sphere.
I warn you now . . .
Do not come near.

If you should choose
To disregard
My wise advice,
You'll find it hard
To extricate
Yourself from mud,
Or disengage
The jaws of Sludd.

I'm Thankful for the Sunshine

I'm thankful for the sunshine,
The mountains and the sea,
I'm thankful that I'm happy,
I'm thankful that I'm me.
I'm thankful for my parents,
My neighbors, and my friends,
I'm thankful for this dinner,
And hope it never ends.

I'm thankful for the pudding,
And that I lick the pot,
I'm thankful for my brother,
Though not an awful lot.
But mostly I am thankful,
It pleases me to say,
That I am not a turkey
This fine Thanksgiving Day.

When I Ride My Rhinoceros

When I ride my rhinoceros,
Which I do every day,
Tigers never bother me,
Gorillas keep at bay.
Cheetahs do not take the chance
Of chasing after me.
Hippos are respectful,
And hyenas let me be.

I'm practically invincible
When I am on his back.
Packs of wolves are wary,
Grizzly bears don't dare attack.
The most ferocious lion prides
Stay fairly far away
When I ride my rhinoceros,
Which I do every day.

Dear Monster of Loch Ness

Dear monster of Loch Ness,
You're not at your address,
We haven't seen you recently,
We miss you, more or less.
We wonder day and night
Why you are out of sight.
Dear monster, we sincerely hope
That everything's all right.

We like it when you're here,
And when you're not, we fear
That nothing will be fine until
You somehow reappear.
We openly confess
You're causing us distress.
For you we yearn, so please return,
Dear monster of Loch Ness.

I Sailed Away to Neverwhen

I sailed away to Neverwhen,
A land that can't exist.
I arrived before I started
On a ship I'm sure I missed.
In fact, I've a suspicion
I did not arrive at all,
Unless I did . . . in any case,
I simply can't recall.

There wasn't much to do there,
And there wasn't much to see,
So everything that happened
Is mysterious to me.
I stayed there for a while or less,
As I had thought I would,
Then left in no great hurry,
Twice as quickly as I could.

I don't remenber very much
About my wondrous trip,
Except that when I sailed for home,
Once more I missed the ship.
However, I am almost glad
I went to Neverwhen,
So if I have another chance,
I won't go back again.

The Walking Talkers

We are the Walking Talkers,
And though we love to talk,
We only talk while walking,
And so we walk and walk.
We talk to one another
In voices loud and clear,
Not minding that we're earless,
And simply cannot hear.

We are the Walking Talkers,
We talk both day and night.
It might appear ridiculous,
But it is our delight.
We do not know a lot of words,
We only know a few,
Yet talk and walk and walk and talk
Is all we ever do.

The Niddlenudds

The Niddlenudds live in a state
Of infinite confusion,
Without an indication
Of the things they'd like to do.
They are in a constant muddle,
They're bewildered, they're befuddled,
For they never have a notion,
Not an inkling, not a clue.

The Niddlenudds meander,
Bumping into one another,
Always saying, "Please excuse me"
And "It's perfectly all right."
The Niddlenudds are loved by all
Who ever come across them,
For though they are oblivious,
They're overly polite.

It's Mother's Day

It's Mother's Day, so I will make
My mother a delicious cake,
A cake no other cake can match,
A cake that I'll create from scratch.
My cake is bound to be a dream,
I'm mixing butter, eggs, and cream,
And milk and sugar, flour and spice,
Spaghetti, raisins, nuts, and rice.

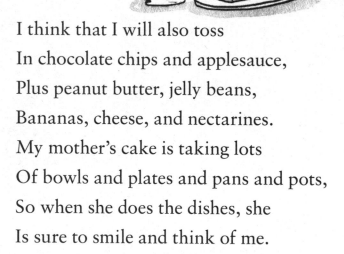

I think that I will also toss
In chocolate chips and applesauce,
Plus peanut butter, jelly beans,
Bananas, cheese, and nectarines.
My mother's cake is taking lots
Of bowls and plates and pans and pots,
So when she does the dishes, she
Is sure to smile and think of me.

Whenever I Chew Bubble Gum

Whenever I chew bubble gum,
I blow a giant bubble.
It's often so enormous
That it gets me into trouble.
I can't seem to control it,
It just grows and grows and grows,
Becoming so colossal
That I cannot see my toes.

It quickly lifts me off the ground,
Sometimes a mile or two.
I thrash around with no idea
Of what I ought to do.
So now when I chew bubble gum,
I'll use some common sense,
And pop that bubble with a pin
Before it grows immense.

If You Fail

If you fail to use your brain,
And confront a speeding train,
You will suffer in a way
Guaranteed to ruin your day.

If You Saw Yourself

If you saw yourself in half,
Folks are almost sure to laugh
At your two divided minds,
And your pair of half behinds.

I Have a Gnu

I have a gnu that's not too new,
It's older than before.
It's obvious my gnu is not
A new gnu anymore.

My gnu is less new every day,
It's normal for a gnu.
And I have heard a rumor
That it's true for people too.

The Lazy Slothrush

The lazy SLOTHRUSH, lacking zest,
Is disinclined to build a nest.
Atop a tree it grips a bough
And manages to sleep somehow.
Its sleep is long, its sleep is deep,
Apparently, it loves to sleep.
Upon its perch, both night and day,
It snoozes half its time away.

The lazy SLOTHRUSH, lacking vim,
When it awakens on its limb,
Makes no attempt to spread its wings,
But yawns a bit and gaily sings.
Its song is lilting, sweet, and high,
It charms whoever happens by.
We're glad to hear its cheery sound,
And hope theSLOTHRUSH sticks around.

SLAW-thrush

My Elephant Is Clever

My elephant is clever,
And dearly loves to play,
So when we are together,
We play throughout the day.

The game he loves the most is fetch,
Which makes it hard for me.
He never just returns the stick . . .
He brings me back a tree.

Nellie

Nellie ate a jingle bell.
She won't say why, we don't know how.
Her stomach rings both day and night—
She's known as Jingle Belly now.

There Are Things Out There

There are things out there in the void of space
We've yet to learn about.
Some may resemble volleyballs
Or have a six-foot snout.
They may be cold, they may be hot,
They may be huge or small.
They may be kind, they may be not,
They may not care at all.

Perhaps one has a thousand arms
And malice in its heart.
Perhaps its dire intention
Is to rip our limbs apart.
Perhaps one plans to turn us
Into mounds of cookie dough.
We don't know what's in outer space,
We simply do not know.

Aan Aaaardvaark

Aan aaaardvaark is aan aanimaal
Thaat feaasts aall daay on aants,
So when aan aaaardvaark is aaround,
Aants haardly staand aa chaance.

Aan aant laacks aany future
If aan aaaardvaark is aabout.
You're saafe if you aare not aan aant . . .
But if you aare, waatch out!

A Chicken on a Mountaintop

A chicken on a mountaintop
Was at a total loss.
She felt a need to cross a street—
There was no street to cross.

That chicken didn't fret too long
But simply used her head,
And sat and sat and sat and sat,
And laid an egg instead.

I Built a Singing Robot

I built a singing robot
That makes everyone rejoice.
They feel honored just to listen
To my robot's wondrous voice.
That voice is truly beautiful,
It's rich and sweet and clear,
The sort of voice an audience
Is jubilant to hear.

Now early every morning,
When my robot sings aloud,
My house is soon surrounded
By an animated crowd.
Some are friends and neighbors,
Others come from far away,
All to hear my gifted robot
Sing a song to start their day.

Tallulah

Tallulah sipped a spoon of glue,
The reason's unrevealed.
She simply can't explain it—
It seems her lips are sealed.

I Do Not Live on Scary Lane

I do not live on Scary Lane,
Where ghastly shadows dance,
Where choruses of spectral owls
Perform unearthly chants,
Where trees are things of menace
And aswarm with savage birds,
Where snakes hiss unintelligible,
Incoherent words.

I do not live on Scary Lane,
Where dragons munch on bones,
Where goblins interrupt your dreams
With terrifying moans,
Where skeletons and gargoyles shriek,
As if they were in pain—
I'm grateful that I do not live
On scary Scary Lane.

If I Didn't Have a Nose

If I didn't have a nose,
I would surely fail to smell.
If I didn't have a voice,
I would surely never yell.

If I didn't have a tooth,
I would surely fail to bite.
If I didn't have a thought,
I would probably still write.

Index of Poem Titles

Index of First Lines

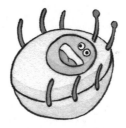